THE OL

EYE

OF THE

CYCLAW

ROBIN PRICE

THE OLYMPUSS GAMES
BOOK II: EYE OF THE CYCLAW

First published by Mogzilla in 2014

Paperback edition:
ISBN: 978-1-906132-83-5

www.mogzilla.co.uk

Printed in the UK

Author's dedication:
'For Scarlet and Indigo.'

Illustrator's dedication:
'For Lorna, Brendan and Barney.'

THE STORY SO FAR...

The OLYMPUSS GAMES series is set in ancient Rome where cats rule the world and people have never existed.

The first book in the series is called: SON OF SPARTAPUSS.

The SON OF SPARTAPUSS (or 'S.O.S.' for short) is a young ginger cat from the Land of the Kitons (Britain). He has just moved to Rome with his mother.

At the market he meets FURIA, a mysterious cat with orange eyes. S.O.S. buys FURIA at the auction, but she is far more expensive than he thinks. When S.O.S. can't pay, the seller calls the guards. S.O.S. is fined ten silver coins. An old cat called FATHER FELINIOUS offers to pay the fine if S.O.S. joins his gladiator school: THE SCHOOL FOR STRAYS.

When he learns that FELINIOUS is FURIA's new owner, S.O.S. agrees to go. FURIA escapes from the school but gets caught. Along with PUSSPERO and MAXI, FURIA and S.O.S. fight their first gladiator battle together. Furia defeats a giant from Cattage.

THE SECRET DIARY OF S.O.S.

MAUIS XXX

May 30th

Dear mother, by the time you read this, I will be on my way to The Olympuss games, in the land of the Squeaks. I'm writing to tell you that I am sorry for running off. I hope you are not too cross. The Emperor gets bored very easily. So this year he has decided to make the games more dangerous than usual. I might not come back in one piece, so I have written down my story in this diary.

Your loving son,

S.O.S

P.S. I'm sorry about that impression of you that I used to do. You know, the one where I went: "Miaow miaow miaow miaow miaow miaow miaow miaow miaow!" I know you hated it, but you have to admit it was seriously funny.

The School for Strays is a tough school. From the grey dawn till the red sun sets we have to practise in the hot sun with our swords and spears. But not today. Today, Maxipuss and I were lazing on purple 'winners' cushions. We sipped cream from golden 'winners' cups and counted our winnings, (paid in biscuits, treats and fish).

If you have read my first scroll, you will know why I was purring like a kitten in a cream shop. The day before, I had won my first victory as a gladiator. As I watched the rest of the school working their claws blunt in the burning sun, I could hear the booming voice of Wulfren, our instructor. He was shouting insults as usual. Stuff about them being as useful as a straw helmet on a battlefield. On the far side of the courtyard sat Father Felinious, the owner of the school. Maxi raised his golden cup and waved at him.

"Your gladiators salute you Father! Thanks for all the fish!"

Now you might wonder why Father Felinious was wasting his best cream and cod on Maxipuss and me. The Father, as everyone called him, was no fool. He wanted the rest of the students to see us living like kings for a day. He was sending out a message. The winners get the cream, but the losers get dirty water and dry biscuits. Every coin has two sides, as my friend Pusspero would say.

Sitting there on that cold morning, I thought I knew everything there was to know about gladiators. In my head I was the king of the Coliseum. But in fact, I had only won a fight at a private party at a senator's villa. His wife could have chosen dancing birds as entertainment, but instead she decided to have a gladiator show. It was a team battle, put on to impress the Ambassador of Cattage.

The Ambassador decided that two Roman fighters should take on one fighter from Cattage. That is why I got to fight my first battle with Maxipuss, the hulk of ginger fur who was sitting next to me, tearing into a plateful of fish.

Maxi is one of those annoying cats who is brilliant at everything they turn their paw to. I would never admit it. But if it wasn't for Maxi, I might not have won my first gladiator fight.

I could not help feeling a bit uncomfortable. I felt bad watching the others working hard whilst I sat around doing nothing. Maxi was not troubled by thoughts like this. He was loving it!

"Hey Liccus! You heard Wulfren. Keep your blade up. And put your back into it!" he laughed.

Then he turned to me and smiled. "This is the life Spartan," he laughed. "Here's to winning!"

I hated the nickname 'Spartan' as much as Maxi loved it. I had foolishly let slip that my father used to work in a spa and is called Spartapuss. From then on, the whole school had started calling me 'Spartan' or 'Flea Hundred' (because of the three hundred Spartan warriors who held the pass at the battle of Furmopolae.)

"Talking of winners," I began, "where's Furia? She should be here. She was the one who defeated the giant from Cattage."

"Furia's being punished because she ran away from school," he said.

"I'm off to find her," I said. "Coming?"

"Are you serious Spartan?" asked Maxi. "It's not every day you get to watch Lucca and Herc slug it out. Let's enjoy it."

I was just thinking about getting up from my cushion when Tigra, one of our instructors, appeared. She was holding something unusual in her paw.

"Paws' Jaws! What's that?" asked Maxi.

She studied us intensely for a moment.

Tigra had a way of looking at you that made you think she was just about to pounce on you.

"Follow me and find out," she said.

Wulfren called the practice to a halt and got all of the students together.

I noticed that Tigra was holding a basket

full of leaves. They glittered like fire in the angry midday sun.

"See these leaves?" said Tigra. "Wulfren and I will be watching you very carefully. If you fight well in practice, you will be given one of these. Wear your leaf in your collar, so that you can be identified for the trials."

"They're made of gold!" shouted Herc in excitement. "I bet those things are worth a few denarii!"

"They are made of bronze," said Wulfren drily. "In case any of you thieving rats are getting ideas."

"Their value cannot be counted in coins," said Tigra. "They are beyond price."

Wulfren paced slowly down the ranks holding the tiny leaf in his enormous paw. "This bronze leaf is an ancient badge of honour...," he began.

He stopped next to Clawdia. The more serious her instructors were, the more likely Clawdia was to mess around. Wulfren let out a low hiss and shook his head slowly.

"Some of you mice do not know the meaning of honour."

Tigra drew herself up to her full height and held up one of the bronze leaves. The bright metal gleamed in the sun.

"Students of the School for Strays..." she began. "You might not have heard of the bronze leaf, but that does not matter. All you need to do is train hard, fight bravely and win."

"And then what?" asked Maxi.

"That is all you need to know for now," growled Wulfren.

"If you are given a leaf, wear it at all times," added Tigra.

Later on, the canteen was buzzing with talk of the mysterious bronze leaves.

"The try outs start tomorrow," said Maxi. "But what are we trying out for?"

"Who knows?" laughed Herc. "Wolfie wouldn't say."

"Probably something painful," laughed Clawdia, licking her bowl. "Did you see the look he gave us? He had a face like a slapped squid."

Whilst the others helped themselves to seconds, I decided to find Furia. There had been no sign of her all day. I searched the school from one end to the other, but she was nowhere to be found. The guards on the gate kept looking at me with suspicious eyes. I didn't want to be accused of trying to escape from school. I was about to give up when I spotted a wooden cage in the corner of the practice arena. At the back of the cage, sat a familiar figure, wearing an iron chain on her leg.

"Furia!" I cried. "What are you doing out here?"

"Eating treats with Queen Candmeet of the Kushionites!" she hissed. "What do you think I'm doing?"

She kicked out in frustration, rattling the iron chain. Then she sank down into the sand with a hiss.

"But I don't understand," I said. "Why are they punishing you? You won the fight.

You beat the giant, didn't you?"

The moon hung in the dark sky like a silver claw. Finally, Furia spoke.

"I ran away from school, remember?"

"I see that you are wearing the charm I gave you," I said, wanting to change the subject.

On her collar, she was wearing the golden charm that I had found on the day of the fight at the villa. "I'm sorry it didn't bring you good luck," I said.

Furia touched the charm. Then she stalked towards me, thrusting it towards my face. The pale metal gleamed in the moonlight.

"Where did you find this?" she demanded.

"Er... it kind of fell from the sky," I replied.

As quick as summer rain, she sprang towards the bars. I crashed to the ground and felt the weight of her chain around my neck. Somehow, she'd managed to trip me and loop the chain around my throat. Now she was pulling it tight and, as the iron chain dug in, I began to choke and splutter.

"No more games," she spat. "Where did you get it? Answer me!"

I spluttered and coughed as the chain tightened around my throat. It was choking the life out of me. I struggled desperately to get free, but she had me like a puppy on a lead.

"Where???" she demanded again. I felt the chain go loose for a moment as she allowed me to answer.

"Here..." I coughed. "Here... At the school..."

"Liar!" she hissed, pulling the chain tight again.

The next voice I heard was Tigra's.

"Spartan! Wake up!" called the tall instructor.

The stars seemed to be drifting gently down the river of the night. Each point of fire got brighter and dimmer as it bobbed along. I rubbed my eyes. Then I rubbed my throat. Finally, I got slowly to my feet.

"Spartan! Are you alright?" demanded Tigra.

"Don't call me Spartan..." I coughed. "My father used to work in a Spa..."

"Never mind that," she snapped. "What

is going on?"

I thought hard for a moment, panicking.

"Explain yourself!" demanded the instructor.

"It was a... choke hold!" I spluttered. "I bet Furia that she couldn't do a choke hold. And... it looks like she won the bet."

"Really?" asked Tigra.

Tigra glared at Furia suspiciously. Furia glared back at her, as silent as a tomb. Without another word, the instructor took something from her pocket and threw it into the cage.

"A bronze leaf!" I cried in excitement. "You're giving Furia a bronze leaf!"

Tigra opened the cage door.

Furia still didn't speak. She stared at the leaf but didn't touch it.

"Put it on," ordered Tigra. "You are wanted for the trials tomorrow and you won't get in without it."

"Try outs? Can I come?" I asked.

Tigra shook her head.

"I wouldn't advise it," she said. "Save the choke holds for the arena. You might not wake up next time."

MAUIS XXI
May 21st

The next morning I woke early and padded down to the canteen. It was empty. I spotted old Pusspero, sitting alone by the window.

"Where is everyone?" I asked.

"Training," he replied.

It seemed that the whole school had decided to make an early start. The idea of winning a bronze leaf had gripped everyone's imagination.

"Pusspero," I began, "I want to ask you something. What's so special about these bronze leaves? Have you heard of them before?"

Pusspero smiled.

"This school is all about winning and losing. Whatever the prize may be, the cats in this place will want it," he said.

As the two of us made our way to the training field, we were interrupted by an excited Clawdia.

"I've got one! I've got one!" she cried.

On her collar, I spotted a shiny bronze leaf.

I should have felt happy for Clawdia. But instead, I was gripped with jealousy. As soon as I saw that leaf, I wanted it.

"How did you get that?" I asked.

Clawdia hesitated. Without answering, she barged past and rushed off to show it to the others.

That morning, the training was intense. Tigra made us run lap after lap around the practice arena. I am no athlete. After three laps, my lungs were on fire and my legs felt like lumps of clay. I wanted to give up. Only one thing drove me on – the dream of winning that glittering prize.

That morning Maxi and Herc were

the best at all the activities. Herc is a brilliant athlete. That cat could balance on a spider's web. No one was surprised when Wulfren gave him a leaf.

When the midday sun was high in the sky, the instructors told us to take a rest. I limped down to the canteen. There I was greeted by the familiar voice of Maxi.

"Hey Spartan!" he called. "Got one of these yet?"

He waved his paw in my face.

"Taaa da da da!" he laughed, opening his paw to reveal a tooth pick.

I let out a groan.

"I got you there didn't I Flea Hundred?" he laughed.

I nodded.

"For a moment, I thought..." I began.

"You thought it was one of these," he laughed.

In his other paw, he held a bronze leaf.

"For Peus sake!" I hissed. "You too? Everyone has got their paws on one except me."

"Students!" boomed a familiar voice. It was Wulfren. "Those of you with bronze leaves, follow me."

I watched in despair as Herc, Clawdia, Maxi and a few others padded off behind Wulfren. Each one of them wore a leaf on their collar with pride.

I wanted to be happy for them. But I could not find any happiness inside me. I felt like a total failure.

"Still here lad?" asked Pusspero.

"Obviously," I hissed. "How do you think that a loser like me is going to get his paws on a bronze leaf?"

"So you REALLY want to go with them?" he asked. "Even though you don't know what it means. We used to have a saying in the army, 'The nail that sticks up gets...'"

"...hammered down!" I hissed, finishing his sentence for him. "I know it. You've told me that a hundred times before."

"The truth is a dish you can serve again and again," said Pusspero.

I wasn't in the mood for Pusspero and his wise sayings. So, without another word, I turned and padded off towards the door.

"Wait!" he called. "You'll need this."

From a leather bag around his neck, he drew out an object and threw it towards me. As it looped through the air, the light danced on it. I knew what it was.

"A bronze leaf!" I gasped. "Pusspero! Where in the name of Paws did you get it?"

"I won it lad," he answered. "A long time ago, when I was a competitor."

"Competitor?" I asked. "Competitor for what?"

"Run!" he said. "Run and you'll catch them up."

"Thank you!" I cried.

"The Sons of Mars never forget a favour," he said. "You helped me at the villa, when I was too ill to fight. Now it's my turn."

I flew out of the canteen like a stone from a slingshot. But where were the others? There was no sign of them.

Skidding to a halt, I stood blinking in the sun. It was a real pad scorcher. You could see the hot air swirling above the red sand.

I sat listening to the sound of my own heartbeat. The sounds paraded past my ears. Two birds were fighting over a worm. The guards on the watchtower were having an argument and the cleaners were washing up the breakfast bowls. Then I heard the sound of a gate creaking open.

"Hades' Hallway," I cried. "That's where they must be going!"

I tore away like a fish off a hook. I shot round the back of the kitchen, knocking over some empty oil jars. The cooks shouted curses after me. At last, I spotted the group. They'd already reached the gates of the practice arena that we call 'Hades' Hallway'. My lungs were bursting as I struggled to make up the ground. The wooden gates squeaked as they started to close. I threw myself at the gap... and came to a slamming halt. The gates had shut. I was stuck outside.

"Let me in! Let me in!" I cried. But it was no use. No one on the other side could hear me calling.

I cursed myself for being a slow runner. Then I cursed Pusspero for wasting my time. If the old fool had given me the bronze leaf instead of droning on with advice, then I wouldn't be in this mess.

Then I felt guilty about that last thought.

The gate was made of an enormous hunk of oak. The walls were made of stone.

I could hear voices on the other side of the wall. I didn't need to listen hard to pick out Wulfren's deep voice.

Cursing, I backed away from the gate. Then I rocked on my back legs and ran at it. The leap carried me a third of the way up. The wood was old and it was easy enough to grip. Digging my claws in, I scrambled up until I was draped over the top of the wall, wobbling like a see-saw. Looking down felt strange. I'd never climbed this high before. But, as any cat will tell you, climbing up is never hard, it's climbing down that's the problem.

Far below, I spotted the Father. I noticed that he had a bald patch of fur behind his ear. Next to him was an immensely fat cat with a face like a bruised apple. He was dressed in plain white with a golden collar. He took a silver bottle from his pocket. He poured oil from the bottle into a bowl and lit it. Tongues of fire leapt up.

"Silence! Father Felinious is going to speak," said Tigra.

It was no use watching the show from up here on the wall. So I inched my way over the ledge. The only way to get down was to run down the wall, digging my claws in and jump the last part. I'd seen this done before, but I'd never tried it myself.

"Welcome to our honoured guest!" said Father Felinious, nodding at the cat in the white robe. "Tell them why they are here."

"Gladiators! You are here because you have been chosen to wear the bronze leaf..." said Wulfren. He left a long pause here, as if it pained him to say this.

Arching my back, I moved myself in position for the descent.

"We are gathered here by the Fire of Olympuss, to find champions..."

Far below, the flame flickered in the bowl. It was a long way down. They say you have to stare fear in the face, but this was madness.

"You are the best that the School for Strays has to offer..."

At that moment I lost my hold and I dropped like a stone, yowling as I fell.

When I landed and the dust cleared I was staring into the eyes of a furious Tigra.

"Some of you have come, even though you were not invited..." she hissed.

The cat in the white robe frowned and looked at Wulfren. The instructor sprang towards me. But before he could open his mouth to speak, I pulled out the bronze leaf that Pusspero had given me earlier.

Tigra frowned. The cat in the white robes beckoned to me and I padded slowly towards him. He examined my bronze leaf.

"How did you get this?" he asked.

My brain raced like a chariot at the

circus. But when I opened my mouth, I found myself telling the truth.

"It was given to me," I said.

"Who gave that to YOU?" boomed Wulfren, looking at me suspiciously.

"Someone who believes in me," I hissed.

"Leave us!" growled Wulfren.

"Wait!" said the cat in the white toga. "All those who wear the bronze leaf have the right to compete. That is the law of Mount Olympuss. He has the right to stay."

"Carry on Wulfren," said the Father.

"Each of you wears the bronze leaf, but your next challenge is to qualify. There are only three places. The team will leave immediately after the final challenge."

"Places? Places for what?" I asked.

"Places for The Olympuss games!" said the cat in the white. "That is why you are here. We must find competitors."

"Any more questions?" asked Tigra.

Then Clawdia spoke.

"The Olympuss games are held in the Land of the Squeaks," she said. "Why are Romans entering?"

Tigra gave her a stern look but the cat in the white toga waved this away with a paw.

"The Squeaks welcome visitors at the games. Ever since the first Olympuss games eight hundred years ago, Romans, and cats from many lands have taken part."

Father Felinious coughed.

"Your Emperor doesn't want you to take part. He wants you to WIN for the glory of Rome."

There was a loud laugh from somewhere in the group.

'What's so funny?' demanded Wulfren.

"What if we don't want the 'honour' of winning for Rome?" sneered Furia.

"Save it Furia!" warned Herc. "Some of us are proud to be Roman. Don't bite the paw that feeds you."

"Well said!" laughed the Father. "And if Rome is not worth fighting for, how about the chance to win one of these?"

From his belt he pulled a sword. But it wasn't the usual wooden sword that he carried. It blazed like the sun.

"A golden gladius?" gasped Maxi. "The Emperor's gone squeaking mad."

"A mad Emperor? In Rome?" laughed Furia. "That would be a first."

"Shut up Hisspanian!" hissed Herc, beginning to bristle.

"Quiet Furia," whispered Maxi. "Talk like that and you'll end up in a sack in the river Tiber with only a brick for company."

"Any more questions?" asked the cat in the white robes. "We have a long day ahead of us."

"I have a question," said Furia, fixing him with her amber eyes. "The Olympuss games used to be about running and jumping, tree climbing and so on.

Why have swords as prizes? Why send gladiators to the games? Why not athletes?"

The cat in white looked rather embarrassed. After a long pause, he answered the question.

"The games were getting old fashioned. So the Emperor is bringing them up to date. Not everyone at Mount Olympuss agrees with the changes. But this year's games are going to be the most 'exciting' games ever.

Father Felinious laughed.

"What sort of changes?" asked Maxi.

"You'll find out," muttered Wulfren.

"The new games need a tougher sort of champion," said the cat in the white.

"Look no further!" said Maxi, stepping forward.

"Don't worry, the Olympuss spirit lives on," laughed the Father. He flipped a silver coin up into the air. "Even if you don't win the golden gladius, every cat gets one of these for taking part."

"Train hard!" said the Father. "The try outs begin tomorrow. In three days time, the winners will leave for The Olympuss games!"

The flame danced. Black smoke rose from the silver bowl. The passion spread around the group like a wild fire. All of us dreamed of winning a golden gladius. All of us, apart from one.

Tigra pointed towards the middle of the arena. When she gave the signal, we rushed into the arena, all except Furia.

"Furia!" said Tigra, shaking her head. "What are you waiting for?"

"Sorry!" said Furia. "I cannot take part. I seem to have lost my bronze leaf."

"What have you done with it!" hissed Tigra.

Furia didn't answer.

Clawdia, who was standing beside me, began to shuffle nervously.

"Clawdia!" I whispered. "Did Furia give you her..."

"SSSHHH!!!" hissed Clawdia. "I promised I wouldn't tell anyone."

Furia smiled defiantly.

"She cannot take part without a bronze leaf," said the cat in the white.

Furia smiled triumphantly. But Father Felinious unclipped the bronze leaf that he was wearing.

"Fortune is with you Furia," said the Father. "You can borrow mine."

He clipped the leaf onto her collar.

Then he gave the signal for training to begin.

MAUIS XXII

May 22nd

Yesterday's training was hard. Wulfren put us through our paces. I started off feeling confident but, by the end of the session, my dreams of a golden gladius had been trampled into the sand. The others were far better than me. At this rate, I wouldn't win a place at the local circus, never mind the Olympuss games. I was starting to feel really sorry for myself when Wulfren called us over for a talk. Maxi and Herc, who were the fastest runners, trotted up to see what he wanted. The instructor fixed them with a stern stare.

"Some of you are looking pleased with yourselves," he began.

"By the look of you, anyone would think that you'd already qualified for the Olympuss games."

Maxi looked guilty. It was true. He and Herc had been cruising all day.

"Well think again!" growled Wulfren. His voice boomed back at us from the far wall of the courtyard.

"The Father has invited some old students to come back and compete against you. So you'll have to beat the best in order to book your ticket to Mount Olympuss!"

That evening, over steaming bowls of roast chicken, the others talked about prizes. Maxi said that winning a sword was an insult to the spirit of the games. But Herc said he thought that there was more gold in a golden gladius than in a golden vine leaf.

No one knew where the Olympuss games were being held this year. Would it be at the ancient hill of Krownus? Clawdia reckoned they would be held in a shed in Hisspania.

Everyone was talking about the ex-students who were coming back to compete against us. Would it be Tyranta the whip or Kitonipuss the great? Whilst this talk was going on, I decided to look for Furia.

Outside, the hunter's moon was high in the sky. Suddenly, a familiar hiss drew my eyes towards a spot in the shadows.

"Furia!" I hissed. "Is that you?"

"No, it's Helen of Tray!" she hissed.

"What did you do with your bronze leaf?" I asked. "Did you really lose it? Or did you give it to Clawdia?"

"Why ask a question if you know the answer already?" she replied.

"Why don't you want to go to the games?" I asked.

"I won't fight for Rome. And I won't fight for Father Felinious either."

She stepped out of the shadow into a pool of moonlight. Her amber eyes were flaming with an intense fire.

"Ssssh!" she ordered.

She held up the golden charm I'd given her before her fight against the giant from Cattage. She wore my present on her collar next to her own charm. The two looked as if they had been crafted by the same paw. Furia held the charm up in the moonlight.

"What did you mean when you said it fell from the sky?" she demanded.

"I meant exactly what I said," I replied.

"I was training on the Octopus (Wulfren's favourite machine). I slipped and went belly up. When I stuck out my sword to protect my face, it clanged against the machine. I blinked. Something bounced off my whiskers. I put out my paw and grabbed it. I couldn't understand where it had come from. It seemed to have dropped from the sky."

"What happened next?" asked Furia.

"Wulfren turned off the machine. I thought he was going to take the charm from me. But he didn't spot it."

"You found it HERE? In the school?" gasped Furia. "That can't be possible."

Her fiery eyes seemed to have gone out.

"Believe me Furia. It is true. Apart from the fight at the villa, I have not left the School for Strays for weeks."

She looked puzzled. The fact that she doubted my word made me annoyed.

"In case you haven't noticed," I said, "this school is guarded. There's a wall and the watchtower and guards. They might be no problem to a ghost like you, but most of us can't walk through walls."

"Follow me," she said.

So I followed her past the watchtower, being careful not to attract the attention of the guards. They'd just had a big fish supper, so it wasn't hard to sneak past without being spotted.

Moments later we were standing on the spot where Wulfren kept the Octopus. It was the most difficult machine we used in our training. Many a gladiator had been defeated by its whirling wooden blades. Hades Hallway was out of bounds. Furia wasn't bothered, but I didn't want to lose the chance to have a try out for the games.

Furia examined the machine, studying its wheels, ropes and levers.

"What are we doing?" I asked.

"Looking," she replied.

"What are we looking FOR?" I moaned.

"Look with your eyes, not your mouth." she hissed.

I took a good look at the battered old machine. Running my paw along the edge of a wheel, the wood felt ancient. The machine had taken a hammering. There were plenty of dents on it, but no markings. At least, none that my eyes could see.

"Get down on the ground," ordered Furia.

"Why?" I gasped.

"Do it!" she hissed.

I fell onto my back looking at the stars.

"Is that the position?" she demanded.

"What?" I moaned.

"Is that where you were sitting when the ring fell from the sky?" she snapped.

Lying would be a better word for it than 'sitting'. Wulfren's machine had nearly rolled right over me. I was sprawling on my back.

"I think I was about here," I said, moving myself into the right spot.

"Look at the machine again. Can you see anything?" she demanded.

There was nothing unusual there. The blade of the wooden sword. A few ropes and levers.

"Furia," I said. "Tell me what is going on. How can I help unless I know what I am looking for?"

"Stars of Asteria!" she hissed. "All right. I will tell you."

The night birds were singing under the temple lamps. Insects buzzed. The only silent thing about the night was Furia. Even though she had just promised to tell me what was going on, she'd suddenly shut up like a clam.

"Furia," I began. "When I first met you at the market, you spoke in Squeak, not Catin. Do you come from the Land of the Squeaks?"

"I am of the Hellenes," she whispered. "The Roman's call us 'Squeaks' because to them, we are tame little mice. But they stole from us. Our music, our buildings and our stories. Our mighty Peus with his lightning bolt became the Roman's Mewpiter."

She'd used more words in the last sentence than she'd spoken in all the time I'd known her. It was as if a different cat was sitting in front of me. Furia from Hisspania had vanished. Who was this?

"Listen to my tale," she said. "My

grandmother was very wise."

"So was mine," I said.

"Yes. But I don't mean she was 'wise' because she knew how to put up a tent in a storm, or she had a good recipe for fish stew – although both those things are true as well."

She leaned even closer and lowered her voice to the faintest whisper.

"My grandmother was a student of the great philosopher Herodicat. She knew all there is to know about maths and geometry. When she saw a thing, she had to know how it worked. And she could make amazing things, with her own paws. It is said that she knew more about the world than ANY other cat under the stars."

As Furia spoke, I admit that I felt jealous. My grandmother was a hot head from the land of the Kitons. She got banished from our village for cheating in a tree climbing contest. She wasn't the student of a philosopher. She used to study the chariot racing results, that was about all.

Furia drew her eyes towards mine and spoke again in a hushed voice, almost a whisper.

"When my grandmother died, she left a message for me. I have to find the four straybos."

'Straybos?" I asked.

"Look," she said touching the two golden charms on her collar.

The charms, or 'straybos' as she called them, looked like tiny wheels with little teeth. Close up, the gold looked a bit disappointing. It was a golden colour all right, but it wasn't really gleaming. It had crossed my mind that the charms weren't actually made of gold. But I decided that I'd better not mention it. Furia seemed to be very proud of her straybos.

"What happens when you find all four of these straybos?" I asked.

"I don't know. But finding them was my grandmother's final wish. I must honour her memory. I must find the four straybos, or die in the attempt."

The jealousy I felt did not stop. How I wished that I had a quest like this!

"Speak a word of this and I will end your life, she hissed. "With each charm, there is a message. What can you see? Any markings? Symbols? Anything like that?"

I examined the machine carefully, looking for signs of anything unusual. I could not find anything.

"I can't see anything like that here." I said sadly.

Furia let out a disappointed yowl. Then, I heard it.

"Ssshhh!" I gasped.

I could hear a ticking noise. It was quiet, but to my ears, it was quite distinctive.

"What?" demanded Furia.

"I can hear something. Listen!"

Suddenly, the ticking stopped. I noticed that a tiny door had opened in the side of the machine. Excitedly, I thrust my paw inside. I could feel something inside the drawer – it was scrap of paper.

Then I heard Furia screaming behind me.

"Spy! Spy!!!" she hissed.

At the same moment there was a rattling noise and the machine sprang into life. The bags of sand began to rise and fall. Its wheels began to turn. Slowly, the machine began to crawl forwards, like a great wooden beetle.

In a panic, I tried to roll out from underneath the machine. But the rows of wooden swords were swishing through the air as the machine came at me. I scrambled back, ducking to dodge the whirring wooden blades. But I was too late. One of the blades connected with my face, knocking me backwards.

"Furia!" I screamed. "Help me!"

But Furia had other things on her mind.

"Spy!" she hissed again. "Somebody sent you! Who was it? Speak or you will regret it."

She had a figure by the tail, and her paws were going towards its throat.

"Furia!" I begged. "Help me! Switch this thing off!"

"Turn the wheel!" called the stranger.

"Turn it! It will stop the machine."

Furia looked towards me. After what seemed like an age, she let go of the stranger and turned the wheel. The machine ground slowly to a halt. The stranger spluttered and coughed, and then staggered forward. For the first time, I caught sight of his face.

"Maxi!" I cried. "For Peus sake! What are you doing here?"

"I saw you leaving our room. I thought you'd come out for some extra practice so I followed you," explained Maxi.

Furia let out a low hiss. The fur on the back of her neck was standing up.

"What did you hear?" she demanded.

"Nothing," said Maxi, backing away from her.

"Liar!" she spat.

"Well... I could not help overhearing something about 'straybos'. And you having two of them. And about you being from the land of the Squeaks and everything."

Furia's eyes were on fire again. I thought she was going to kill him on the spot. But instead she told him to go on talking.

"Listen Furia," said Maxi. "I love the Squeaks. I grew up listening to all the stories: the wooden horse of Tray, the one eyed Cyclaw, the golden fleas and all the other myths. Ask the Spartan. He'll tell you."

Maxi turned pleadingly towards me.

"It's true Furia," I said. "He never stops talking about the Squeak myths. He can quote from Socates and everything."

I wasn't sure about this last part but I thought it might help.

"Enough!!! hissed Furia. Open your mouth again Spartan, and I swear I will close it."

Maxi got up and started to brush the sand out of his shiny coat.

"Listen Furia," he said, with a little bit of the old confidence coming back into his voice. "I can help you on your quest."

When I heard this, I began to bristle.

"Hey..." I began.

Maxi put his paws up apologetically.

"I mean, WE can help you... The Spartan and I," he explained. "We'll find the other two charms and... if there happens to be any treasure at the end, we can share it.

Actually, I don't want any treasure. I'm only in it for the quest."

"Are you? Are you really?!!?" raged Furia. She was as angry as a bag of rats.

I felt angry too. I wanted to help Furia. Me! Not Maxi. He was saying all the wrong things. It had taken weeks for me to win Furia's trust. Now he was ruining everything.

Furia stepped towards Maxi. Like a striking snake, she shot out her paw and knocked him to the ground. Then she seized Maxi by the throat. I thought she was going to choke the life out of him there and then.

Suddenly a familiar voice boomed out.

"Drop him!"

A blow like a hammer knocked Furia away from Maxi. She skulked back into the corner, licking her wounds.

"Klaws' jaws!" roared Wulfren. "What in the name of Chaos are you three doing?"

There was a long silence.

"We're.. training..." I said hurriedly. "We wanted to do some extra training. For the Olympuss games..."

"Training?" laughed Wulfren. "You'll

need it. You two! Get your claws off my machine and get back to your baskets."

Maxi and I nodded.

"Sorry Doctor!" said Maxi. "I hope this won't affect my chances of qualifying tomorrow."

"I wouldn't pack your bag for Mount Olympuss just yet," said Wulfren.

He dismissed us with a wave of the paw. Maxi padded off in the direction of the canteen. Furia stalked after him.

"Not you!" cried Wulfren, ordering her to stop. "Furia, you're coming with me. I'm going to keep you out of trouble."

First Arrow

As I padded off into the night after Maxi, I held something in my paw. It was the scrap of paper that I'd pulled out of the secret drawer in the machine.

If you were holding a scrap of paper in your paw with a secret on it, would you look at it? Of course you would. Me too! But that night something stopped me. I had a feeling that this was Furia's quest. She should be the first one to see what was written on it. So I left the paper in my pocket.

Maxi was unusually quiet as we padded back to our sleeping area. He didn't get into his basket, he sat there like a statue, gazing out into the darkness. After a long silence, he spoke.

"Do you think she'll let us join the quest?"

"If I were you, I would drop the whole thing about 'the quest'. This is Furia's mystery."

"I know," said Maxi.

He let out a low sigh and his tail began to flick.

"What's the matter?" I asked.

"You might find this really hard to believe coming from a cat like me," he began. "But I'm kind of..."

He paused, searching for the right word.

"Jealous?" I suggested.

Maxi looked at me in amazement.

"Yes Spartan, I'm jealous," he said, "you've hit the target with your first arrow! I'm jealous of Furia. I would give my right paw to have a quest like hers. A cat of my talents is wasted here at the school. I need a challenge like Purrseus and all the other heroes."

I sighed. Maxi and I were always competing over things. Both of us wanted to go on Furia's quest.

"I've been waiting for something like this to happen all of my life," sighed Maxi.

"Don't get your hopes up," I said quietly. "Furia doesn't want any help."

His smile broke like a wave on the beach.

"There's always the Olympuss games," I said. "You might even win yourself a golden gladius."

"Well said!" he replied. His face had brightened. "Thanks Spartan. It's good having you on my team."

I tried not to bristle. Why did it have to be Maxi's team? He could not join in anything without taking over.

I put my paw in my pocket and smiled. There was still something Maxi didn't know about. I desperately wanted to know what was written on that mysterious scrap of paper that I'd found in the Octopuss. But I wasn't going to share it with Maxi.

MAUIS XXIII

May 23rd

The Day of the Trials

The next morning, I found myself waiting in Hades Hallway with the other competitors. The chances that any one of us would make it to the Olympuss games were small. I had joined the chosen ones, the ones who had been given a bronze leaf. My dream of glory at the Olympuss games was still alive.

I took in the strange scene before us. The courtyard was packed with all manner of unusual equipment. Gladiator gear is strange enough. We dress like the ancient heroes. We wear helmets shaped like fish and visors that you cannot see out of! But this equipment was even stranger. There were ladders and wires, hooks and poles, arrows and jars of fire. In the centre of the arena were three enormous pine trees. But there were no leaves on the pines. Their branches were completely bare.

The students stared at the trees with puzzled expressions. All except two of us – Maxi and I were looking for Furia.

"She's not here!" hissed Maxi. "I told you she would run away again."

The flame of Olympuss was already alight. All the other students were chattering excitedly at the sight of the strange game that was set out before them. I spotted a lone figure, sulking behind a rack of spears. Maxi had seen her too. Without another word, we both raced towards her.

"Furia!" called Maxi. "You made it. We have so much to discuss. I've been thinking about your quest..."

Furia hissed and glared at Maxi.

"Silence in the ranks," boomed Wulfren. "Listen carefully, if you ever want to win your place at Mount Olympuss."

Tigra padded forward. It was so quiet, you could have heard a feather fall.

"There are many different events at the Olympuss games," she began. "This first challenge will test your climbing skills."

Maxi looked disappointed.

"They said there would be changes," he said. "But what sort of game is THIS?"

"It's called the tree climb," said Tigra. "See the golden bird at the top of each tree? The first one to bring back two birds is the winner. Understood?"

"Understood!" said Maxi.

"Oh and one more thing," said Tigra. If you fall, you will be eliminated. That means there will be no Squeak holiday for you. There are no second chances from now on."

Wulfren produced an old leather bag from his pocket.

"Step forward if we call your name," he boomed.

The tension was unbearable.

"Hercatules," he called.

"That's me!" said Herc, stepping shakily forward.

"You will be competing against..." he began.

"Maxipuss!" announced Tigra, drawing a name from her bag.

"Going up against these two will be one of our ex-students," said a voice. It was Father Felinious. "Welcome back Hoppa."

Beside the Father stood a wiry looking creature. He was as thin as a spear and his green eyes flicked from left to right like a lizard on a fly hunt.

"Hoppa?"said Clawdia. "Not Hoppa the Squeak?"

"The very same," laughed the Father. "The undefeated winner of thirty two gladiator contests. Net-cat extraordinare."

A trumpet sounded. Father Felinious had hired a band for this practice event. The three competitors made their way towards the practice arena.

"Good luck Maxi," I called.

"I don't wait for luck Spartan," he laughed. "I've dedicated my life to this."

Maxi looked at Hoppa and flashed the jugulare sign (a claw across the throat that signalled 'death' in the arena).

Hoppa's thirty two victories in the ring obviously didn't impress Maxi.

The challenge looked simple enough. Three trees, three cats, three golden birds. The first cat to bring back two golden birds would be the winner. It was a test of wits, speed, and climbing skills.

The trumpets fell silent. The drummer held his drum stick high in the air. Father Felinious padded over to the Olympuss flame and the cat in the white lit a red candle.

"When the smoke turns red, the contest will be over," he said.

Hoppa stared up at the tree, muttering something under his breath.

"Remember, if you fall, you lose,"

warned the Father.

Maxi leaned back on his haunches, getting ready to spring. With a crash of cymbals, the game began. Each cat flew towards his tree like an arrow from a bow. Herc was fast but Maxi was faster. He reached his tree in a heartbeat. Hoppa was the last to arrive, but once he started climbing, he was frighteningly quick. Hoppa had already decided which branches would give him the fastest route up the tree, whilst Maxi and Herc were making their minds up as they climbed.

Maxi sprang from branch to branch. He is no stranger to the cream bowl, and the thin branches creaked as the big cat set his weight upon them. Herc was still in the lead, but Hoppa was gaining on him. Soon Herc was only two branches away from the top of his tree.

"Hercatules! Hercatules!" shouted Herc's supporters. He landed on the final branch and reached up for the golden bird. But there was a sharp snap and the branch gave way. Herc tumbled down the tree, twisting as he fell. Unable to stop himself, he yowled helplessly as the red ground came rushing towards him.

"Eliminated!" called Wulfren. A cymbal crash rang around the arena.

Now there were only two competitors left.

As I was watching Herc's fall, Maxi had grabbed his first golden bird. Now he was climbing back down as fast as he could.

"Bad luck Herc!" called Maxi, as he reached the bottom and delivered the bird.

"Curse my luck!" hissed Herc. "Fortune has got it in for me."

"What happened?" called Maxi, turning back to face the tree.

"The branch gave way," yelled Herc.

"I reckon you had too many stuffed dormice last night," laughed Maxi.

By now, Hoppa had grabbed his first bird and delivered it. Now he switched to Herc's tree and went looking for a second bird. The branches barely wobbled as he stepped on them. Slowly but surely, he was pulling ahead of Maxi.

"Faster Maxi! He's in the lead!" called a voice from the crowd.

Maxi let out a hiss and sprang up over to Herc's tree. He reached the top just before Hoppa and grabbed the golden bird.

But when he put his weight on the branch, it gave way instantly. Maxi was about to fall. He would have been eliminated, but his quick reactions saved him. He shot out his left paw and caught hold of another branch, about half way down the tree.

"Miiiiaaaoooowww!" he moaned.

But he still had the golden bird, clamped

between his teeth as he clung on by the tips of his claws.

"Flea brained fool!" laughed Hoppa, seeing Maxi in trouble. He hadn't forgotten that Maxi had flashed the jugulare sign at him earlier.

Hoppa wasn't having any problems with his branches. With a laugh, he sped down the tree towards Maxi.

Maxi hung there in despair. He was dangling at a point about halfway down the trunk of the tree. Far below him was the red dust of the arena floor. He could hear the excited shouts of the crowd below.

"Jump! Jump! Jump!" yelled the crowd, who had a cruel sense of humour.

I didn't join in with these taunts, but I didn't exactly cheer Maxi on either.

"Swing! Swing back to the other tree," called a cracked old voice. It was Pusspero.

"What are you doing here?" I whispered.

"I sneaked in," he said. "I wouldn't miss this for all the fleas in Fleagypt."

"Swing over lad! Swing back onto your tree," advised Pusspero.

Maxi hung there for a moment, like

a rabbit on a butcher's hook. Then it dawned on him. Pusspero was telling him to change trees. One of the branches on the other pine was just within reach. Maxi let out a yowl and began to swing faster and faster. Finally he let go and flew through the air like a giant ginger squirrel.

It wasn't an elegant landing. Maxi crashed into the tree with a thud. The branches creaked and shuddered. Meanwhile, Hoppa was right behind. He reached out a paw trying to knock the golden bird from Maxi's jaws. But Maxi refused to let go.

The thin pine swayed like a sapling in a hurricane. Hoppa wobbled, let out a hiss and fell wailing from his perch. He hit the ground with a dull thud.

The cymbal crashed out again.

"Eliminated!" said Maxi coolly, beating Father Felinious to it. "This means, I'm the winner, right?"

Wulfren nodded. Red smoke billowed from the candle and hung in the still air.

"So that's it! I've qualified!" yelled Maxi triumphantly.

The cat in the white toga nodded.

"Can I come down now?" asked Maxi.

May 24th

Second Place

Maxi has become completely unbearable since he won a place in the team which will go to The Olympuss games. He's acting as if he is a champion with a golden gladius in his paw already! Today the other students staged a re-creation of his victory against Hoppa, in the canteen. There is one good thing about Maxi's victory. Perhaps it will take his mind off Furia's mysterious quest. Hopefully he'll be so busy training for the Games that he'll have forgotten all about Furia. I've decided to sneak off and find her.

White Sheet

A second entry tonight. I went to see Furia, as I'd planned. The moon was rising as I crept out of my room and padded across the courtyard. The whole school was asleep. There was not a single sound to be heard under the cold stars. Not even the cry of an owl or the whisper of the spring wind.

I finally found Furia by the east wall. When I explained about the paper that I had pulled out of the secret drawer in the machine, her eyes caught fire.

"Why didn't you show this to me before?" she demanded.

"Maxi was there." I moaned. "I thought you'd want to keep it secret."

Furia hissed and padded towards me.

"That's why I've come now," I said. "To give it to you now, in private. I thought that you should be the first one to open it."

Backing away, I offered her the paper. I thought she was going to tear it out of my paws.

Furia grabbed the paper and ran a claw across the seal, ripping it open.

Standing in a pool of spring moonlight, she looked like a statue. A grey-furred goddess, carved in stone.

When she had studied the paper, she let out a low hiss, spun around and stalked away into the night. The paper floated gently to the mosaic floor. I retrieved it and held it up. What was the message? What was written there? Was this the start of the Quest? I had to know.

But when I opened the paper, there was nothing on it. It was completely blank. I felt the anger rise up from the tips of my claws. Maxi had the Olympuss games. But there was nothing for me. I thrust the paper back into my pocket, and cried under the cold stars.

MAUIS XXV

May 25th

Running Rats

The next morning broke like they always do. And as any wise cat will tell you, things always look different in the light of dawn. This was the second day of the trials. Perhaps Fortune would spin me a good one today, (as my Father would say). Like Pusspero, my dear father is full of sayings.

'If at first you don't succeed... give up' is my favourite. He told me that if you are going to fail at something, then it's better to fail quickly than waste your life chasing a mouse you can never catch.

"Come on Spartan!" called a voice. It was Maxi. How long would it be before he mentioned the fact that he had qualified, and I had not? I gave it three flicks of the tail.

"Better get a move on!" he said, "You won't qualify for the games lying there in your basket."

Three flicks of the tail was about right.

The yellow sun was climbing the steps of the sky temple as we made our way towards Hades Hallway.

"I wonder what old Wolfie has in store for you this time?" said Maxi. "Whatever happens, fight hard! Never give up! Take life by the throat and shake it," he said.

"Maxi, why are you coming?" I asked. "I mean, you're through to the games already. Why should you come today?"

"I wouldn't miss this for all the treats in Tray," he laughed. "Besides, Furia will be there. We need to talk about her quest."

My heart sank like a brick as I remembered the disappointment of the blank paper. A second wave of gloom hit me when I realised that Maxi had not forgotten about Furia's quest. The

Olympuss games were not enough for him, it seemed.

Maxi and I were amongst the last to arrive at the gate. The trumpet was sounding as we slipped through the door. The Father stood next to the cat in the white robe. Wulfren and Tigra waited impatiently for the chatter to die down.

"The wolf looks pleased with himself," said Maxi. "That means you're in for it Spartan."

"Students of the School for Strays," said the Father. "This is the second day of the trials. Today you will ALL get a chance to qualify. Wulfren will explain."

The hulk of an instructor stepped forward. Maxi was right, Wulfren DID look pleased with himself. That meant that something painful was about to happen.

"Rats!" roared Wulfren. But for once he was not insulting us. All around the arena guards stood ready. Each guard had a sack and a large vase. I noticed that the sacks were wriggling.

On Wulfren's command, the guards emptied the sacks. Soon the arena floor was a sea of rats.

"Somewhere amongst that lot, is a rat with a golden tail," said Wulfren.

"The goldie!" cried Liccus.

"If you want to call it that," sighed Tigra, "I cannot stop you."

The group laughed.

"All you need to do is catch the golden rat," explained Wulfren.

"Golden birds, and now rats with golden tails," said Pusspero. "What's going on?"

"It's the Emperor Nero," said Clawdia. "He's gold mad. They say he's building a golden house, with a golden floor and a golden lake and a golden pond and golden bee hives."

I tried to picture it, but I couldn't imagine owning that much gold.

"I had a pet rat once," whispered Lucca.

"What happened to it?" asked Clawdia.

"My grandmother baked it in a pie," said Lucca.

As Wulfren waited for the chatter to die down, I looked around. Surely it could not be as simple as this.

"One more thing," said the cat in the white robes. "This is Fortune's game. Use these."

Tigra opened a case and gave each of us a black cloth.

"What do we do with these?" I asked.

"You wear them over your eyes," said Tigra.

"How can we see if it's the golden rat if we are wearing these?" moaned Liccus.

"That's the point, you half-wit!" hissed Clawdia.

The cat in the white toga produced a candle from his pocket, touched it to the flame and lit it.

"The blue smoke will signal that time is up," said Tigra. "Anyone holding the wrong rat at the end of the game will be..."

"Eliminated!" said Lucca. "We get it."

"How will we see the blue smoke, when we're wearing these?" asked Clawdia.

"I expect they'll sound a trumpet or a tuba or something," I said.

I slipped the blindfold over my eyes. The darkness was perfect.

I heard the frantic squeaking of the frightened rats as they dashed left and right. I could not see the fire, but I could feel the heat. And then I heard a sudden whoosh. The guards had poured out oil from their vases. The floor of the arena was criss-crossed by rivers of orange flames.

I felt a bump as something scrambled over my tail, and then another bump, and another. The rats were squeaking in terror. They hadn't liked the sacks, but they could not stand the flames.

Suddenly, something piled into me. I was knocked to the floor like a skittle.

"Sorry!" said Lucca.

"Mew three times if you want to quit," said Wulfren.

Something ran over my tail again. I stuck

out a paw, but it was impossible to catch.

"This is madness!" I moaned. "Why are we trying to do this blindfolded?"

"It's blind Fortune," called Maxi. "Fortune always wears a veil. That's why you're all wearing blindfolds."

"Thanks for the history lesson," groaned Lucca, lunging at another rat and missing.

I felt a stab of pain in my tail.

"Miaaowwch! One of them just bit me!" I moaned.

"Mine used to do that," said Lucca. "I called him Nippa."

I padded carefully over to my left, well away from where I thought Lucca was standing. Then I prepared to make a grab for the next rat to come past. Lying completely still with outstretched paws, I waited until something touched my paw and then I flipped it into the air.

It worked. I heard a squeal as the rat somersaulted through the air. Lunging forward, I snapped with my mouth. But I was biting into thin air. Then I heard a thump and a scrabbling noise as the rat ran off. I could smell something bitter. I began to choke. Then I realised that my own coat was on fire.

"Miaaaaouuuch!" I cried, frantically rolling around in the dust to put the fire out. "That hurts."

Cursing, I waited for the next rat to come racing past and got ready to pounce. This time I flipped too soon. Just the tip of its claw connected with my paw as I flipped it up. It escaped, squealing like a rusty wheel.

"Don't give up!" called a cracked voice. "You nearly had it."

It was Pusspero. "Quick Spartan! Try again," he called.

Crouched low, I waited silently for the next rat to pass. I sensed it before it arrived. Flipping it up with my paw, I heard it squeak and zoomed in on the sound. Lunging forward, I caught it in my jaws. As soon as I bit down, I felt it. The tail was cold and hard and tasted of metal. I'd done it! I'd caught the rat with the golden tail!

I was paralysed with fear. What if I dropped it? I was so close to qualifying. I could not stand another disappointment.

But the big golden rat didn't want to be caught. It let out an outraged squeak. Then it wriggled desperately. Swinging itself up by its tail, it lashed out and bit down hard on my nose.

The pain was unbearable. I let out a yell of agony. And as soon as I opened my mouth to scream, the rat broke free and shot off.

From behind me, I heard a shout of excitement. "I... I think I've got it!" cried Lucca in ecstasy.

As the trumpet sounded, my heart sank like a stone. Wearily, I pulled the blindfold from my face. My coat was badly singed from the fire. Blue smoke rose from the candle, the signal that the game was over. So that was my chance gone. I had come so close. I had held the golden rat in my teeth!

But I'd failed the final test.

"Oh!" said Lucca, examining the rat that he'd caught as the game had ended. "This one isn't the golden rat. What does that mean again?"

"It means that you're eliminated!" growled Wulfren.

Laughter rang out around the arena. If there was a competition for fluff brains, Lucca would win the golden gladius every time.

Rat Trap

I padded quickly back towards the canteen. I was trying hard to avoid Maxi.

Pusspero caught up with me.

"Don't be down hearted lad," he said.

"That's actually the worst thing you can say when someone is downhearted," I muttered. "You may as well tell a starving stray to stop feeling hungry."

Pusspero fixed me with a hard stare.

"Listen lad," he said. "The trials are not over yet. No one caught the golden rat, so it means there's two places up for grabs tomorrow."

"Two places or ten thousand places," I muttered. "What's the difference?"

I wanted to get past this, but ripples of regret kept reminding me.

"I had victory by the tail Pusspero," I moaned.

The old cat looked over his shoulder.

"Sometimes these things happen for a reason," he said. "In the Sons of Mars, we had a saying..."

"Another saying?" I moaned. "Go on!"

"Well, actually we didn't have a saying for everything," he sighed.

I couldn't help smiling.

"Thanks Pusspero," I said. I thrust my paws into my pockets, about to slink off. Then my claw caught on something.

"My mind's gone blank," he said.

I remembered the scrap of blank paper in my pocket. On a whim, I pulled it out.

"What have you got there?" he asked. But I did not answer. I was staring at the paper. Something amazing had happened.

"Writing!" I gasped. "Where did that come from?"

I looked up at the skies. Were the gods

toying with me like a mouse?

"The paper!" I said. "It was blank completely blank before. But now it's covered in writing."

"Let me see," said Pusspero.

I gave him the paper, but then I pulled it back again.

"Sorry Pusspero," I explained. "But it's not a message for us. I don't think we should read it."

"Suit yourself," said the old soldier.

I knew that I had to find Furia so I took off towards her sleeping quarters. She wasn't in her basket, so I searched the school. The sun was high in the sky and I couldn't risk missing the final day's trials. Reluctantly, I made my way towards Hades' Hallway and rushed through the gate.

There was a buzz of excitement about the place.

"Is he here yet?" asked a voice.

"Duh! Of course he's here!" hissed Clawdia.

"He's the most famous gladiator ever to set paw in the arena," said Liccus.

"I think we'd notice if he was here!"

laughed Maxi.

But I wasn't paying attention to this chatter. I'd spotted someone at the back, slumped on a pile of cushions.

Taking care not to attract Maxi's attention, I nonchalantly padded over.

"Furia!!!" I called.

"Leave me alone," she hissed.

"Look! Look at this," I said, fumbling in my pocket for the scrap of paper.

Suddenly, a trumpet rang out. Father Felinious and the cat in the white toga entered the practice arena. They were followed by Wulfren and Tigra.

"Students of the School for Strays. Today is the last day of the trials for the Olympuss games. There are two places left..."

I turned to Furia and gave her the paper.

"What use it that?" said Furia. "Leave me alone. Get back to your games."

"Read it," I said. "Look at it again. There is writing on the page now. When I pulled it out of my pocket earlier, I saw it."

Furia's orange eyes went wide with wonder. She snatched the paper and studied it.

"... today we are lucky to welcome back

the most famous fighter that this school has ever produced..." said Father Felinious.

But I wasn't paying attention. My mind was on the mysterious writing.

"What does it say?" I whispered.

Furia passed the paper to me.

"Read it yourself!" she hissed.

Suddenly, the trumpet sounded again. There was a roar from the crowd.

I unfolded the paper and read.

The answer is two times two...

Tick tock tick
climb the white tip mount
time runs out
Olympuss!

"It's a riddle!" I exclaimed.

"Of course it's a riddle," hissed Furia.

"What does it mean?" I asked.

"Stars of Asteria! How should I know?"

Her tail began to flick. She was already regretting sharing the information with me.

"The answer is two times two..." she said.

"Four!" I said excitedly. "Two times two is four!"

"For Peus sake!" moaned Furia. "We'll have to do better than that."

Suddenly, the trumpet sounded again. There was a gasp from the crowd. The ground shook. The drums began to bang and the trumpets blared. The lyre player played a creamy little run of notes. Suddenly, the sun was blotted out by a shadow. When I turned around, I could not believe my eyes.

"Undefeated champion...Victor of one hundred fights," began Felinious. "It is our privilege to welcome him back to the school. Meet the one-eyed wonder... The Cyclaw!"

Before me stood a brute of a cat. Bigger than Wulfren, bigger than the giant from Cattage. On his arm he held a shield bearing the emblem of an eye. In his paw, he wielded a club the size of an oak branch.

The crowd went wild. Well, some of them were a bit wild already. They stared at the legend as if he was Mewpiter himself come down from Mount Olympuss.

Furia didn't join in. She was too busy

trying to work out the riddle.

"What does that line about 'the white tip mount' mean?" asked Furia. "Could it be a horse?"

Before I could answer, Wulfren spoke.

"To book your place at the Olympuss games, you must escape from the Cyclaw," explained Wulfren. "Do you see the two golden eyes that are hanging from his belt? Unhook an eye, bring it back and you will win a place."

"This is the last chance you'll get," said Tigra. "There are only two places left. Who wants to go first?"

"Come on mice! Don't be shy. Who's first?" demanded Wulfren.

The cat in the white toga padded slowly over to the bowl of fire and produced a candle from his pocket. Carefully, he touched the candle to the fire. It was not long before the flames began to take hold.

"When the green smoke rises, the game is over," he explained.

The mighty Cyclaw stood in the middle of his island. He held his club at the ready. The dying rays of the sun bounced off his bronze helmet.

The Cyclaw shuffled from paw to paw.

No one volunteered to face him. I was about to put my paw up, but I felt an iron grip around my wrist.

"Pusspero?" I said. "What are you doing?"

"Stopping you from going first lad," he explained. "Let the others make the mistakes. Learn at their expense."

"I can't stand it any longer," said Liccus. "I'm going to have a go."

The crowd gasped. This was an unexpected turn of events.

"Liccus! Liccus!" chanted the crowd.

The black and white cat padded slowly forwards. The practice arena had been rigged out with ropes and posts. The competitors entered a little door leading to a walkway. On the other side was the 'cave' of the Cyclaw. The idea was that you had to enter the 'cave', slip past the Cyclaw, unhook a golden eye and make it back. If you fell into the blue area, you lost the game.

The Cyclaw nodded under his enormous helmet. In the middle of the grill was a gap that made it look like he had a single lidless eye.

"Wait!" said the Father. "Give Liccus a helmet and armour."

As Wulfren strapped Liccus into the armour, I nudged Furia.

"What can it mean?" I whispered (thinking about the riddle).

Maxi, who had come up to stand next to us, misunderstood my question.

"The Cyclaws lived on an island," he said. "That's why they've marked out the area in blue. It's the sea. The Cyclaws weren't the cleverest of monsters. They could not swim and they didn't even know how to build boats. That's why they couldn't chase Odyssipuss after he blinded their leader."

"The Cyclaw only had one eye, right?" I said, playing for time.

"That's right Spartan!" he laughed. "Our friend over there lost one of his eyes in battle. That's why he got the nickname Cyclaw."

Wulfren finished doing up Liccus' armour. It was made of thick leather, with padding underneath. A bronze helmet completed the outfit.

"Now you're ready," said Tigra.

"Bring us back a golden eye for dinner," called a voice.

Liccus padded slowly along the walkway that led to the 'cave' of the Cyclaw.

He stepped off the rope onto the platform. He only came up to the knees of the mighty cat. The two golden eyes dangled from the monster's belt.

Liccus waited. His fur was standing on

end and his legs were trembling.

"Get on with it!" called a voice. "The rest of us want a go as well!"

Liccus inched closer. For a moment, it seemed as if the Cyclaw could not see him. Having worn a heavy helmet myself, I knew that it was hard to see through the grill. Liccus thrust out his spear, trying to unhook a golden eye. But the Cyclaw spotted his move. He side-stepped to the right and struck like a cobra. His massive club smashed into Liccus' chest and knocked him flying. He crashed into the blue sand with a thud and a groan.

The arena fell silent. Liccus didn't move.

The Cyclaw looked towards Wulfren.

"Eliminated!" announced the tall instructor.

A couple of guards entered the arena and began to drag Liccus out. There was a massive dent in his helmet. His claws left little tracks in the sand.

"Is he dead?" gasped Clawdia.

"He'll live," said Tigra, examining the poor student. "He's just stunned."

"Who's next?" demanded Wulfren. Unsurprisingly, there were no takers.

The cat in the white robe turned to Father Felinious.

"Come on gladiators!" said Wulfren. "Who's next?"

Not one cat volunteered. The Cyclaw watched, as still as a rock in an ocean of sand. He raised his club in the air.

The Father trotted over to Wulfren. I saw them exchanging a few words.

"What can it mean Furia?" I said again. With a sigh, she read the riddle again.

The answer is two times two...

Tick tock tick
climb the white tip mount.
time runs out
Olympuss!

"The answer is two times two." I said again. "It must be something to do with the number four. What do you think Furia?"

Furia didn't answer. She was glaring at Wulfren and Tigra. They were coming to fetch her. In a panic, I thrust the paper back into my pocket.

"It's the Father's orders," said Wulfren.

"That means you have to get in there."

"You can make me go in, but you can't make me win!" said Furia with a smile.

"Shut it!" said Wulfren, ramming the bronze helmet over her head.

Tigra laced up the leather armour.

"Just make it look good, that's all. At least try to unhook an eye," she said.

Furia approached the rope walkway. In her right paw, she held a spear. Ducking, she slipped through the entrance and perched on the walkway.

The Cyclaw waited, sweeping his club across the sand. Two golden eyes hung from his belt.

The crowd gasped as Furia crept slowly towards him.

I felt a paw on my shoulder.

"You've dropped this lad," said Pusspero. He placed the paper with the riddle into my paw. It must have slipped out of my pocket.

I looked at the riddle again.

"The answer is two times two..." I groaned. "What can it mean?"

"It's a code," said Pusspero. "It should be simple enough to crack."

"Simple?" I asked. "What do you mean simple?"

The old solider smiled.

"Because they've given you the key in the poem," he said.

My puzzled expression said it all.

"The key?" I muttered. "What key?"

"It's easy!" said Pusspero. "It's a message in code. Two times two is four. That means you need to read each fourth word in the poem."

I looked at him in amazement.

"We used codes all the time when I was in the army," he explained. "You don't want the enemy reading your messages."

My mind raced like a whipped horse.

"Every fourth word!" I cried. "Pusspero... that means..."

I was interrupted by a gasp from the crowd. In the arena, the Cyclaw was tired of waiting for Furia. Brandishing the club in his paw, he stepped towards her and roared.

"Furia!" I called. "Get the golden eye! You've got to win!"

It was no use. In her heavy bronze helmet, she couldn't hear a word I was saying.

Furia wasn't trying. She didn't want to win a game for the glory of Rome.

Pushing through the crowd, I made my way to the entrance.

"Where do you think you're going?" demanded Tigra.

"Hey Spartan," said Maxi. "Wait your turn!"

He stepped in front of me, blocking my way.

"Let me through!" I said. "I've got to get a message to Furia."

"What message?" he asked.

"There's no time to explain," I hissed. "It's about the quest..."

"Spartan!!!" hissed Wulfren. "Get back here now! Somebody stop him!"

"Stop who?" yelled Maxi, stepping

aside to let me through.

As I trotted along the walkway, I heard Maxi's voice again.

"Hey Spartan! Take this!"

He flung a wooden gladius through the air. Maxipuss has a hard throw. The sword came spinning towards me at eye level. No one was more surprised than me when I caught it. Half of the crowd cheered. The other half laughed at me.

Father Felonious turned towards the cat in the white robe.

"I'm sorry," he said. "I'll stop the game. I'll have the Spartan thrown out!"

"That will not be necessary," said the cat in the white robe. "There are still two places left."

The Father gave the claws up sign.

The crowd roared their approval.

Gasping for breath, I finally arrived at the spot were Furia was standing. The Cyclaw wasn't worried. He picked up a rock from a basket at his side.

"Furia!" I called. "Listen! You've got to win this one."

"No way!" she said. "Not this time!"

"The poem..." I gasped. "It's a code..."
But before I could finish my sentence, I
heard a swooshing noise.

The Cyclaw's club tore through the air
and smashed a rock towards me. I saw it
too late. In a panic, I realised that I was
not wearing a helmet. Suddenly, Furia
flicked out her spear, deflected the rock
and saved my good looks.

The Cyclaw reached for another rock.

"What do you mean?" asked Furia. "What code?"

"Two times two is the answer," I said. "It means you have to read every fourth word. Ignore all the other words."

I heard the swooshing noise again. Another rock shot towards me, as fast as a fisher can let out a fishing line. Furia read the poem out loud.

The answer is two times two...

Tick tock tick
climb the white tip mount
time runs out
Olympuss!

"Every fourth word?" she said. "That's climb... mount... Olympuss!"

This time I saw the rock coming and I protected my face with my sword. When the stone hit the wooden blade, it shattered into pieces.

"The Olympuss Games," I said. "You've got to qualify. The winners leave for Mount Olympuss tomorrow. You've got to win yourself a golden eye."

"No," said Furia.

My heart sank like a stone in a well.

"Not just one eye. We need two."

She smashed away another rock as it came towards my face.

"You're coming with me," she said. "Now help me to get this helmet off."

As I helped her out of the helmet, Furia's amber eyes flashed and her tail flicked impatiently.

"Here, take this!" she said, thrusting the helmet into my paws.

"What do I do with it?" I asked.

"Put it on," she said, "and follow me."

I pulled on the heavy helmet. The world went dark and the shouts of the crowd became muffled. I edged down the path. Through the narrow visor, I saw Furia, confidently stalking towards our opponent. The Cyclaw reached into the bag and picked up another rock. He swung the club again and blasted it towards Furia. But she ducked at the last minute. There was a mighty crash and the world turned over. The stone had hit me in the face.

"Miaooowch!!" I moaned, clutching the helmet.

The crowd clapped and laughed.

"Careful Spartan!" warned Furia.

We edged forward. My heart pounded. After what seemed like an age, we'd made it to a spot on the same level as the Cyclaw. Standing here, it was easy to see why he had won so many victories in the arena. He was built like a prize bull. Turning away from the basket of rocks, he raised his oak club.

He let out a booming laugh and waved the club wildly in the air.

"Where's your helmet gladiator?" he asked.

I was stunned. I was expecting a monster, but he was talking to us as if we were three old friends who had just bumped into each other at a fish stall.

Furia glared at him but she did not answer.

"Tell them to throw her a helmet," he said. "I'm going to beat you, but I don't want to crack her nut."

"Salve Cyclaw!" I said. "My friend Maxi is a big admirer of yours."

The Cyclaw nodded.

"Aren't you going to ask for that helmet?" he said.

Furia shook her head.

"Don't worry, I won't need it," she said softly.

The Cyclaw shook his head slowly.

"I could do with a sword," I said.

"Throw him another blade," he roared.

The crowd cheered. The arena had its heroes and its monsters. The Cyclaw looked like a monster but he'd won a reputation as one as the fairest fighters in the gladiator business.

Somebody threw a gladius into the arena. This time it sailed over my head and I didn't catch it.

"Spartan half wit!" called a voice from the crowd. The drummer began to beat his drum. The Cyclaw shifted from side to side, swinging the club.

"Ready?" asked the Cyclaw.

"Ready!" replied Furia.

In a flash, she darted towards the giant. Her spear flicked towards his helmet. The Cyclaw batted it away with the club but Furia rolled out of the attack, still clutching the spear in her paw.

"You move well" said the Cyclaw, "for a female!"

Furia ran and leaped towards him again.

The club swung at her but she danced away from it. The Cyclaw struck at thin air. I'd seen Furia fight like this before.

I wasn't worried about Furia, but I how was I going to grab a golden eye?

Clouds of dust rose into the hot air. The drums beat wildly and the crowd cheered and hissed. The next time Furia attacked I was ready. Furia leaped towards the giant. The Cyclaw swung his club once more. This time, as soon as he'd swung the weapon, I rolled towards him. The Cyclaw was watching Furia. With a swipe of the sword, I tried to snag the golden eyes. But my blade got caught on the giant's belt.

"You!" hissed the Cyclaw, raising his club ready to strike. Frantically, I tugged at the belt but my sword was stuck.

"Furia!" I called. "I need some help..."

There was a crash and a ringing sound as the mighty club smashed down upon my helmet.

Every time I breathed in I sucked clouds of dust through my visor.

"Aaarrgghh!" roared the giant.

The Cyclaw had struck a blow with his club. But it was a glancing blow.

Somehow, Furia had managed to trip him up.

"Grab his belt!" called Furia. "Get the eyes!"

Reeling, I struggled to my feet and took in the scene before me. The Cyclaw was on the ground, but he could not move. Furia had her spear wedged into the visor of his helmet.

"Quickly!" hissed Furia. "What are you waiting for?"

I stopped trying to free my sword. Then I reached in with my paw and unhooked the two golden eyes from the Cyclaws' belt. As fast as falling rain, Furia raced over to where I was standing. I presented her with one of the eyes. Then the pair of us ran back the way we had come, as the crowd cheered wildly. I looked back but the Cyclaw wasn't following.

Furia padded calmly back down the walkway. She left the arena without saying another word. However, I did not want to leave so quickly. I kissed the golden eye and raised it high into the air. The trumpet rang out. Even the cat in the white robe got up and applauded. I stood with the cheers of my friends ringing in my ears. Somehow, I had qualified. I was going to The Olympuss games.

Milk and Magic

"Farewell ginger!" called a voice. Pusspero had come to the gate to see us leave for the land of the Squeaks. Maxi and Furia were already sitting on the cart. It would take us to the port of Ostia, on the first leg of our long trip to Mount Olympuss.

"I can't believe what I saw today. Magic before my very eyes," I muttered.

"Magic? What magic?" laughed Pusspero.

"The poem," I said. "The paper was blank but then the writing appeared."

"You mean the milk writing?" asked Pusspero. "We used it all the time in the army."

I looked at the old soldier in amazement.

"You had magic milk in the army?" I said, "I find that hard to believe!"

"Just ordinary milk," laughed Pusspero. "You write the message in milk. You can read it when it's wet. But when the milk dries, the message disappears. To read it, you hold it near a flame and the message appears again."

"You used this in the army?" I gasped.

"All the time," said Pusspero. "The barbarians thought it was magic. But it was really just milk."

The red sun was rising as the last of our luggage was loaded onto the cart. I gazed at the old solider, wondering if I'd ever see him again. For years I'd longed to see the sights of Rome, but now I was leaving for the Squeak Islands, on an Olympuss adventure.

"Pusspero, Pusspero!" I laughed, "What made you so wise?"

"Time," said the old soldier.

"What do you mean?" I asked.

"Stay alive Spartan," he laughed. "If you can survive the Olympuss Games, you might find out."

THE OLYMPUSS GAMES

Follow the adventures of Son of Spartapuss and his fiery companion Furia from gladiator school to the foot of Mount Olympuss.

SON OF SPARTAPUSS

BOOK I   ISBN: 9781906132811

New to Rome, the son of Spartapuss (nicknamed S.O.S.) has a lot to learn. When a mysterious stranger pays his debts, he finds himself in a school for gladiators.

EYE OF THE CYCLAW

BOOK II   ISBN: 9781906132835

The Son of Spartapuss discovers that his friend Furia is on a secret quest. Meanwhile, the trials for the Olympuss Games begin. To win a place, S.O.S. must defeat the fearsome gladiator known as The Cyclaw.

MAZE OF THE MINOPAW

BOOK III   ISBN: 9781906132842

On route to the Olympuss Games, the Son of Spartapuss and Furia get mixed up in an ancient mystery. Can they escape from a monstrous danger?

STARS OF OLYMPUSS

BOOK IV   ISBN: 9781906132828

As Furia's quest reaches an end, the Squeaks are holding the biggest games ever. But the Roman Emperor Nero has made some terrifying changes to make the games more exciting.

WWW.MOGZILLA.CO.UK/SHOP